THE QUEEN'S HANDBAG

Steve Antony

To Donald

All rights reserved. Published by Scholastic Press, an imprint of Scholastic Inc., *Publishers since 1920*. SCHOLASTIC, SCHOLASTIC PRESS, and associated logos are trademarks and/or registered trademarks of Scholastic Inc.

The publisher does not have any control over and does not assume any responsibility for author or third-party websites or their content.

No part of this publication may be reproduced, stored in a retrieval system, or transmitted in any form or by any means, electronic, mechanical, photocopying, recording, or otherwise, without written permission of the publisher. For information regarding permission, write to Scholastic Inc., Attention: Permissions Department, 557 Broadway, New York, NY 10012.

Originally published in the UK in 2015 by Hodder Children's Books, a division of Hachette Children's Books, a Hachette UK company

This book is a work of fiction. Names, characters, places, and incidents are either the product of the author's imagination or are used fictitiously, and any resemblance to actual persons, living or dead, business establishments, events, or locales is entirely coincidental.

Library of Congress Cataloging-in-Publication Data Available

ISBN 978-1-338-03293-2

10 9 8 7 6 5 4 3 2 1   17 18 19 20 21

Printed in China 54
First American edition, June 2017

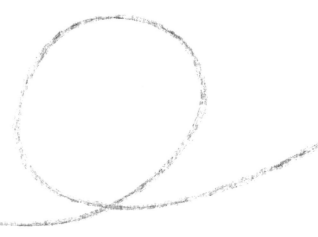

THE QUEEN'S HANDBAG

Steve Antony

Scholastic Press · New York

The Queen was ready for her
tour of **Great Britain** when...

A sneaky swan swooped off with her handbag!

The swan was fast,
but so was the Queen!

She drove after it to . . .

Windsor Castle.

Then she rode after it to . . .

Stonehenge.

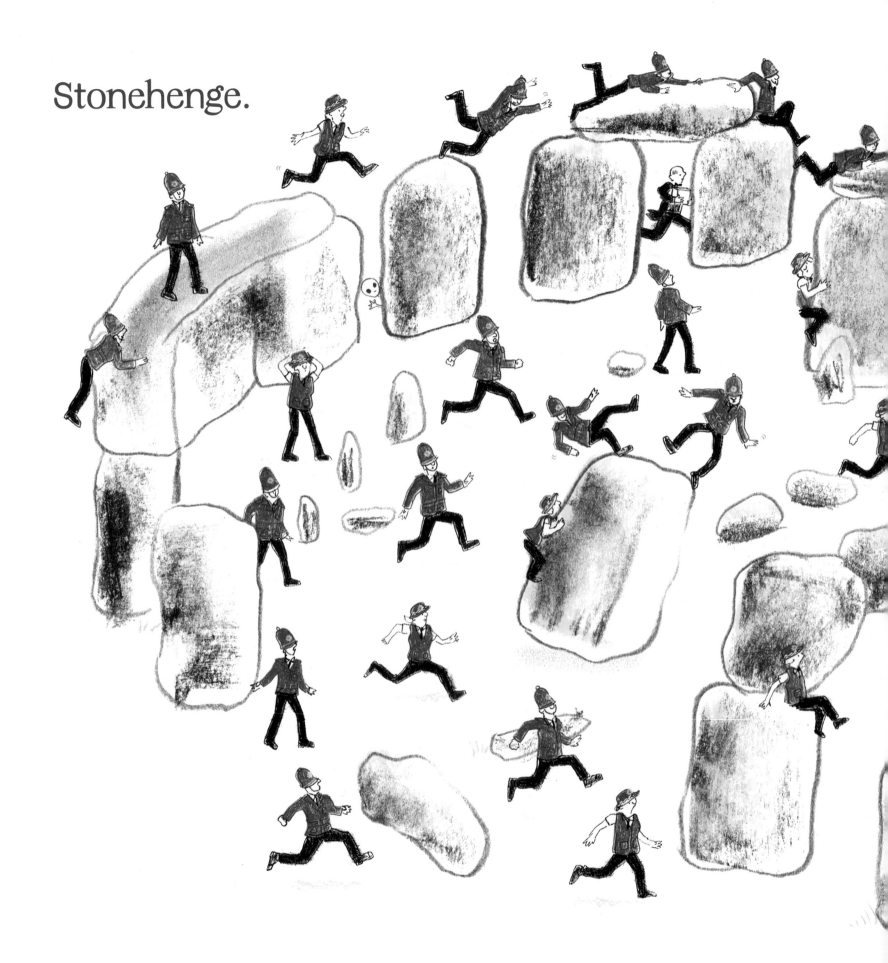

Then she flew after it to . . .

the White Cliffs of Dover.

She cycled after it to . . .

Oxford.

She dived after it to . . .

Snowdonia.

She sped after it to...

the Giant's Causeway.

She chugged after it to . . .

the Angel of the North.

She galloped after it to . . .

Edinburgh Castle,

and all the way back to . . .

London. But the swan was nowhere to be seen,

until the Queen spotted it in . . .

the London Marathon,

where she finally caught the sneaky swan at . . .

...the finish line!

Windsor Castle,
near London, is the Queen's weekend home. More than 500 people live and
work in the castle — more than any other castle in the world!

Stonehenge
is a prehistoric monument built more than 5,000 years ago in
southwest England. It is one of the Seven Wonders of the Medieval World.

The White Cliffs of Dover
are part of the southeastern English coastline and recognizable
by their striking white chalk appearance.

Oxford
is a city northwest of London and is home of the University of Oxford,
the oldest university in the English-speaking world.

Snowdonia
is a national park in north Wales. It has the biggest mountain in the United Kingdom.
Many rare animals live in the park, including feral goats, rainbow leaf beetles, and red kites.

Giant's Causeway
is an area of land along the coast of Northern Ireland that consists of more
than 40,000 basalt columns. It was created during an ancient volcanic eruption.

The Angel of the North
is a sculpture by Sir Antony Gormley, near Newcastle, England.
Made of steel, it is 66 feet tall with wings that are 177 feet wide.

Edinburgh Castle
is a historic fortress on a 430-foot rock in the city of Edinburgh, Scotland.
It was built over an extinct volcano.

The London Marathon
is a long-distance race held in the city of London. It was first run
in 1981 and has been held in the spring every year since.